SUPERHERO SILLINESS

Don't miss

GOOFBALLS #1
The Crazy Case of Missing Thunder

GOOFBALLS #2
The Startling Story of the Stolen Statue

#3

SUPERHERO SILLINESS

by Tony Abbott

illustrated by Colleen Madden

EGMONT
New York USA

EGMONT

We bring stories to life

First published by Egmont USA, 2012
443 Park Avenue South, Suite 806
New York, NY 10016

Text copyright © Tony Abbott, 2012
Illustrations copyright © Colleen Madden, 2012
All rights reserved

1 3 5 7 9 8 6 4 2

www.egmontusa.com
www.goofballsbytonyabbott.blogspot.com
www.greenfrographics.com

THE LIBRARY OF CONGRESS HAS CATALOGED
THE HARDCOVER EDITION AS FOLLOWS:
Abbott, Tony
Superhero silliness / by Tony Abbott;
illustrated by Colleen Madden.
p. cm. -- (Goofballs; 3)
Summary: The Goofballs are invited to a superhero masquerade to
stop a mysterious figure from stealing a priceless collection--
ISBN 978-1-60684-166-2 (hardcover) -- ISBN 978-1-60684-367-3 (pbk)
ISBN 978-1-60684-368-0 (ebook)
[1. Mystery and detective stories. 2. Collectors and collecting--Fiction.
3. Masquerades--Fiction. 4. Stealing--Fiction. 5. Humorous stories.]
I. Title.
PZ7.A1587Sup 2012
[Fic]--dc23
2012025672

Printed in the United States of America

Book design by Alison Chamberlain

To my family,

the superheroes in my life.

—T.A.

Contents

1

First of All

I'm Jeff Bunter, and I'm a Goofball.

A Goofball who loves mysteries.

But it's no mystery how I became a Goofball. I've been one since the beginning of me.

First of all, I didn't cry when I was born.

I burped.

Second of all, when I was two, I got Sparky, my pet corgi. He barks like this: "Goof! Goof!"

Third of all, on my first day of preschool, I decided I was a dog and ate my lunch on the floor.

"Why don't you sit at your desk like everyone else?" my teacher asked me.

"I can't wag my tail when I sit down," I said.

"But Jeff, you don't really have a tail," my teacher said.

"Sure, I do," I said. "It's the tale of a boy who decides he's a dog and eats his lunch on the floor!" The class laughed at that.

"Very goofy, Jeff," the teacher said. "Please take your seat."

"Where should I take it?" I asked.

The class laughed even more.

"Take it to the front of the class and tell us your tale!" said the teacher.

"Goof! Goof!" I said, and the class laughed even louder!

As you can imagine, I made lots of friends that day. I've been making them ever since.

But only three of them are as goofy as me. First of all, there's Brian Rooney. He's an inventor of crazy stuff that doesn't always work but looks cool.

Then there's Kelly Smitts, who has curly blond hair and is very suspicious and very serious.

Finally, there's Mara Lubin, who is as skinny as a stick, wears big green glasses, and loves disguises.

They are the nuttiest friends in the world. Which makes them perfect Goofballs.

Together, we solve mysteries.

Super-mysteries.

Like the one yesterday.

We were at the beginning of a long line of hungry people outside Pizza Palace, waiting for the big clock on the library to strike 12:00 noon. At noon, the doors would open.

It was a big day at Pizza Palace, and it was a big day for the Goofballs. Exactly one year ago, Luigi the baker had named a pizza after us.

The Goofball Pizza has cheese, garlic, pineapple, and peanut butter.

Just listing the toppings makes me hungry.

For the first anniversary of our special pizza, Luigi promised us a new mystery topping.
It was so mysterious, even *we* didn't know what it was.

"Brian, what are you doing?" asked Kelly.

Brian was stretching his jaws open as wide as he could. He looked like a lion ready to swallow his own head.

"Exercises," Brian said. "To see how many slices of pizza I can chew at the same time." He measured his mouth with a ruler he took from his cargo shorts, where he keeps all his inventor junk.

"My record is three slices at once," Brian said. "But today I'm going for four. Tomorrow? Who knows?"

"I do," said Mara. "The hospital!"

The mayor of Badger Point was in line, too. He wore his official top hat. Principal Higgins was also in line. So was Mrs. Bookman, the librarian. It was a long line.

Behind us stood our classmate Billy Carlson with his sister, Millie.

She is the captain of the middle-school gymnastics team.

Billy and Millie. Their names rhyme.

They also have the same red hair. I mean that their hair is the same color red. Not that they share one head of hair. That would be hard, since they go to different schools.

"Mara, what are *you* doing?" asked Kelly.

Mara was squinting into the window of Pizza Palace, first without her glasses, then with them, then without them, then with them.

"Maybe she's trying to discover the mystery ingredient," I said.

"No," said Mara. "I want to see what I look like without glasses. But I need my glasses to see what I look like, so it's not working."

I shook my head. Brian laughed. "That reminds me of the time I tried to look at the back of my head. But I couldn't turn around fast enough. The front of my head was everywhere I looked."

Me? I was jotting down everything in my cluebook. Things like this:

Billy and Millie —
red hair, gymnastics

My cluebook is a small notebook I carry everywhere. Detectives throughout history have written down their clues and used them later to solve mysteries. You never know when clues will come in handy.

Besides that, I was working on a theory.

I was trying to prove that Goofballs are even goofier when they're hungry. So I wrote down what my friends were doing:

Brian — goofy mouth exercises
Mara — wants to see how she
looks without glasses but can't
Kelly — what IS Kelly doing?

"Kelly, what are *you* doing?" I asked.

Kelly power walks everywhere, and right now she was power walking back and forth in front of the restaurant, faster and faster, her arms flying like propellers.

"I'm trying to make time go faster," said Kelly. "So we don't have to wait so long until our next real mystery."

It was true. The only mystery we were solving was the mystery topping on the Anniversary Goofball Pizza.

And that would be solved as soon as the clock struck twelve.

But we never heard the clock striking twelve. Or any other number, either.

Instead we heard something else.

"Pssst!"

Mara giggled. "Someone say 'excuse me.'"

"It wasn't me," Brian said. "I'm empty. I need all my space for pizza—"

"Pssst!" came the sound again.

"Maybe it was Jeff," said Kelly.

"Not me!" I said. "I'm busy writing."

When the sound came a third time—*"Psssssst!"*—we spun around on our heels and saw a tall, skinny man in a funny round hat hiding behind a lamppost.

One long finger was pointing to the four of us. Then the finger curled back as if he wanted us to come over.

And all the while, he kept making noises as if he was losing air.

"Pssst! Pssssss-ssss-sssssst!"

2

Invitation to a Mystery!

The tall skinny man in the funny round hat turned out to be . . .

"Picksniff?" I said.

Picksniff is our friend Randall Crandall's butler. We met them when Randall's pet pony, Thunder, mysteriously went missing.

"May I have a word with you?" whispered Picksniff.

"I hope it's a word we know," said Kelly. "There are a million words in the English language, and we don't know all of them."

The butler frowned. "Several words, then," he said. "And I'll try to make them ones you know. It is a matter of utmost importance."

My mystery-loving ears tingled. So did my fingers. I jotted down those lovely words:

Utmost importance

"Billy and Millie, would you hold our places in line?" I asked. Billy nodded and Millie flipped her big red hair to the other side of her head.

We scurried over to Picksniff.

"Forgive me for using my library voice outside," the butler whispered, leaning close. "But I don't want anyone to hear me."

I could tell that the other Goofballs were as excited as I was. "Go on," I whispered.

"Master Randall has an urgent request for the Goofy Children," Picksniff said.

"Goofballs," said Mara, blinking through her big green glasses.

"Ah, yes." The butler took a tablet computer from his pocket, and when he turned it on, Randall Crandall's face appeared on the screen.

"Hello, friends," said Randall from the tablet's screen. "I'm having a party tonight, and I want you to come to it."

"Wow, thanks," said Kelly. "Is that the urgent request of utmost importance?"

Randall shook his head. "No. I think a mysterious character called the Dutchman will attempt to steal my priceless collection of rare and antique derders."

We stared at one another.

"Picksniff, please turn up the volume," said Brian. "It sounded like he said 'derders.'"

"He *did* say derders," said Picksniff.

"Master Randall's world-class derder collection is the largest collection of derders in the world!"

"You said a bunch of words twice," Kelly said.

"That's how big his collection is!" said Picksniff.

"Wow-wow-wow!" said Mara.

"You can say that again," said Randall.

Whenever anyone says, "You can say that again," we do Rock, Paper, Scissors to see who gets to say it again.

Kelly won. We were all Scissors. She was Rock.

"Wow-wow-wow!" she said.

"Do the Goofkids know what derders are?" asked Picksniff.

Brian practically fell down laughing.
"Of course we do! A derder is the
cardboard tube at the center of a roll of
toilet paper or paper towels or wrapping
paper!"

Brian took a flattened cardboard tube from his cargo shorts and opened it up. "It's called a derder because you can play it like a horn."

He held it up to my ear and said, *"Der-der!"*

I nearly fell down. "Owww!" I said.

"I know, right?" said Brian.

"You Gooflings are smart," said Picksniff.

"We're Goofballs," said Kelly. "Not Gooflings and not Goofy Children. But we *are* smart."

Randall continued. "My grandmother told me legends about the Dutchman and warned me that he might be coming. He is a notorious thief who will stop at nothing to steal my priceless collection. Will you help me?"

It didn't take a second.

It didn't take a fraction of a second.

"Yes!" we all said together.

"Thank you," Randall said with a smile. "I will see you at the party. For now, Picksniff will give you the details. Be careful. Over and out!"

The screen went black.

"Of course we'll do it," I said. "Picksniff, what can you tell us about the Dutchman?"

The butler shook his head slowly. "All we have is this shady photograph that Master Randall's grandmother took long ago."

It was a fuzzy picture of a man in a wide-brimmed hat. All we could see of the Dutchman's face was a long curly mustache.

I sketched the Dutchman in my cluebook.

"I'm afraid the Dutchman's identity is unknown," Picksniff said.

I could have smirked, but I didn't. "Nothing is unknown to the Goofballs," I said.

"What about the future?" asked Brian.

"Except maybe the future," I said.

Picksniff nodded. "Wonderful. Now, listen. Master Randall requests that you come to his party *in*—"

"A pizza box?"

"A hot-air balloon?"

"An old pickup truck?"

"A hurry?"

Picksniff shook his head. "No, no. Master Randall requests that you come *incognito*."

Mara frowned. "Is that an Italian car?"

"Is it the opposite of *outcognito*?" said Brian.

Picksniff grumbled. "No, no. *Incognito* is a Latin word meaning 'in disguise.' Tonight's party is a masquerade!"

Brian raised his hand. "Is a masquerade like lemonade or orangeade or limeade?"

"To answer that, I'll need your derder," I said. When Brian handed it to me, I pressed it to his ear. "NOOOOO!" I yelled.

Brian cried, "Owww!"

"I know, right?" I said.

"A masquerade party is one where the guests dress up," said Picksniff. "Tonight, everyone will come as superheroes. But not famous ones. Brand-new ones. You should come dressed up to blend in."

Mara beamed behind her glasses. "Disguises are my specialty. We'll use my costume shop, otherwise known as my basement."

"I love that place," said Kelly. "I'm already getting ideas for costumes."

"Thank you, Goofnuts," the butler said softly. "I'll be back for you this afternoon." Then he jumped behind the wheel of his block-long limousine and drove away.

Suddenly, Brian gasped. "All those mouth-stretching exercises for nothing. Look!"

When we turned, we saw that it was after the stroke of noon, the line was gone, and all the seats in the restaurant were taken.

"We'll be hungry later!" said Mara.

Which was good for testing my theory but bad for testing my stomach. I tried to be strong.

"At least now we have a real mystery," I said. "So let's go choose our costumes!"

Which is exactly what we did.

3

How Superheroes Are Born

"*Der-der! Der-der-der-derrrrrr!*"

After calling our parents to tell them what we were doing, Brian played marching music through his crumpled derder all the way to Mara's house.

Mara's house *looks* like a normal house, but her basement is bigger than a clothes store. A *weird* clothes store.

There were racks of checked pants, striped shirts, skinny dresses, and fat capes. There were shelves of hats, from top hats to baseball caps to sombreros to helmets made from coffee cans.

"This is super-awesome stuff," said Brian. "Where did you get it all?"

"My mom is the costume lady for a local theater," Mara said. "How do you think I got so fashionable?"

Kelly grinned. "For our superhero disguises, we'll need clothes like these to help us be super-imaginative."

There were counters piled with jars and sticks and brushes for makeup. There were fake beards and mustaches.

Pretend heads modeled every color of wig.

"Look, I'm Billy and Millie," said Brian, dropping a hunk of red hair on his head.

I made a list of some cool superhero disguise stuff in my cluebook:

Green mustache
Striped balloon pants
Purple pirate boots

"The party is in three hours. We'd better get to work," said Mara.

While Brian, Mara, and Kelly scrambled around, I looked through my cluebook.

"We know very little about the Dutchman," I said. "I wish we knew more."

"We know that he's Dutch and a man," said Kelly, holding up a green jumpsuit, frowning, then returning it to the rack.

"At least we have his picture," said Brian.

I studied the photograph. "But is he old or young? Does he work alone or with others?"

Suddenly, Brian yelled, "I'm ready!"

"So soon?" asked Mara.

Brian stood there with a big grin on his face. But that's not all he had on. He wore a pair of puffy pants covered with dozens of pockets, a snug T-shirt, and a fuzzy wristband on each arm. On his head sat a bald cap with ridges of thick white hair over his ears.

"Are you a superhero or a clown?" I asked.

Brian smiled slyly. "The name is Papers. Tommy Papers."

We stared at him.

"Uh . . . *what*?" I said.

Brian grinned, then patted one bulging pocket after another. There was a crunching sound each time. "These pockets are filled with small pieces of paper. Thus the name. Tommy Papers," he explained.

"But *why* are your pockets filled with papers?" Kelly said.

"It's quite simple," Brian said. "In the course of our investigations, we Goofballs could find ourselves being chased by bad guys, could we not?"

"It could happen," said Mara, nodding.

"And if we're being chased by bad guys," Brian said, "they must be very smart."

"How do you figure that?" I asked him.

"Because *we're* very smart," Brian said. "And if the bad guys are that close behind us, they must be smart, too."

I didn't know if that was true, but I liked the way part of it sounded, so I wrote it down:

We're very smart

"Go on," I said.

"So," Brian continued, "if bad guys chase us tonight, I—excuse me, my superhero identity, Tommy—will scribble little notes on the papers. But here's the brilliant part—"

"We're waiting for that part," said Kelly.

"Tommy Papers doesn't scribble a whole message," Brian said. "He only scribbles *part* of a message. Then he throws the paper behind him and runs." He paused.

"And?" I asked.

"Tommy is glad you asked," Brian said. "If, as he has already proved, the bad guys are smart, they'll undoubtedly like to read."

"Anyone who likes to read will have no choice but to gather up all the scraps of paper Tommy tosses behind him and try to piece them together to read his message. When they slow down to do that, it will be easy for the Goofballs to escape. Simple, right?"

We stared at Brian.

We couldn't speak.

"Tommy Papers takes your silence as a yes," he said. "And Tommy says, 'Brilliant!'"

"Does Tommy only talk about himself in the third person?" asked Mara.

Brian smiled. "He does."

"People, we need the ultimate disguises," Kelly grumbled. "We need to catch the culprit, to snare the stealer, to trap the thief, to foil the foe!" She paused. "Foil? Foil! Excuse me!"

Kelly did an about-face and ran upstairs.

"Now *I'm* going to find *my* perfect superhero costume," said Mara. Her hands flew from rack to rack and table to table. In no time, she was a rainbow of layers—shirts, pants, skirts, sweaters, shawls, scarves, and socks, from a pair of baby blue slippers to a bright pink beret with Mara's head beneath it.

"Meet Blazey Blazington!" she said.

"I don't want to," I said, shielding my eyes.

"Maybe you're Crazy Crazington," said Brian. "Your clothes are nutty."

"Which is totally the point," said Mara. "Blazey Blazington is a fashion nightmare. Because I am normally so fashionable, it's the perfect disguise. No one will recognize me."

"Okay," Brian said. "But if you're going to be a superhero with Tommy Papers, you need to have incredible powers. What powers do you have just wearing crazy colors—?"

All at once, Mara twirled like a spinning color wheel. Brian's eyes rolled like marbles until he lost his balance and fell to the floor.

"Whoa!" he cried. "That's crazy!"

"No, that's Blazey," Mara said.
"Blazey Blazington! Your turn, Kelly.
Kelly? Where's Kelly?"

"Here I am!" she said, running down
the stairs and jumping in front of us.
She was covered with aluminum foil
from head to toe.

"Call me . . . InvisiGirl!"

"InvisiGirl?" said Brian. "But we see you right there."

Kelly grinned. "Do you?"

"You're a big shiny thing," said Brian.

"Look," said Kelly. "At a masquerade party, everyone wears great costumes, right?"

"Sometimes super-great costumes," said Mara with a curtsey. "Like someone we know. Hint ... hint ... me!"

"Right," said Kelly. "So when everyone wears a great costume, they can't stop wondering what they look like. So here I come, covered with foil, and what happens?"

I frowned, then I got it. "People look at themselves in the reflection?"

"Exactly!" said Kelly. "With everyone checking themselves out, no one looks at me. And if no one looks at me, I must be . . ."

"Invisible!" I said.

Kelly grinned from ear to ear. "Logical."

"Wow, you are *smart*," said Brian.

"Also logical," said Kelly. "Now, Jeff, it's your turn."

I was the last one. I had to have as great a costume as they had. But with so many clothes to choose from, I couldn't decide.

Suddenly, I spotted a pair of old-man suspenders on the old-man table. Then I attached the suspenders to my pants and put my arms through them.

It came to me in a flash of brilliant brilliance. I hooked my thumbs under the shoulder straps and stuck my elbows out.

"Behold my flashing triangles of power!" I exclaimed, and I waved my bony elbows every which way at blurring speed. Everyone jumped back to avoid the terrible force of my angled weaponry!

"Call me . . . Elbow Johnny," I said.

"And me . . . Blazey Blazington," said Mara.

"And me . . . InvisiGirl," said Kelly.

"And him . . . Tommy Papers," Brian said, pointing to himself.

So we did. It actually took a long time to call each of us our brand-new superhero names, but we finally got it done.

And just in time, too, because the moment we finished—

Beep-ba-beep-beep!

"Goofballs," I said, "our limousine is here!"

4

The Big House

Randall Crandall's super-long limousine was idling in front of Mara's house.

"Splendid outfits," Picksniff said as we approached. "But where is the fourth Goofgirl?"

"Goofball! And I'm right here!" said Kelly, jiggling her foiled hands in front of his face.

Picksniff gasped. "I didn't see you there."

"I know it," said Kelly, then she vanished into the giant backseat.

As we drove to Randall's house, I flipped through the pages of my cluebook. "Picksniff, sir," I said, "I've been thinking."

"What a relief," said Brian. "I was starting to think I had to. Take it away, Elbows."

"Picksniff," I said, "you whispered to us this morning outside Pizza Palace. Do you think the Dutchman is nearby?"

"We cannot be certain, sir," the butler said as we turned up Randall's driveway, which is as long as a road. "The Dutchman reportedly has a vast network of evil helpers.

"Some of them might be listening."

I wrote that down:

Evil helpers . . . listening?

"One has to be very careful,"
Picksniff said. "Master Randall's
collection is simply too valuable to take
chances with."

"You'd be a good Goofbutler," said
Kelly.

"Thank you, miss," said Picksniff.

Minutes later we pulled up at
Randall's giant home and got out of the
extra-long car.

"This is the second biggest house I've
ever seen," Brian said, looking up at
the mansion.

"What's the first biggest house?" I asked.

"This one," he said. "The first time I saw it I was younger, which means I was smaller, which means the house was bigger then."

Kelly, Mara, and I just looked at one another.

"This way to the party," said Picksniff.

We followed the butler up the wide steps to the big front door and into a room twice as huge as the Cafeteri-Audi-Nasium, the giantest room at Badger Point School.

A chandelier as big as a hot-air balloon hung from the ceiling and sparkled over a humongous room filled with odd people.

"Wow!" said Mara. "What a party!"

She could say that again, but it would take too much time, so I kept quiet.

"I know why they call it a ballroom," said Kelly. "You can play a ballgame in it."

"But instead of catching a ball, we'll be catching a thief," I said.

The problem with that was that you could barely see to the far end of the crowded room it was so filled up with people.

"Who are those crusty guys?" asked Brian, pointing to a bunch of paintings of old folks.

"Master Randall's great-grandfathers and great-aunts," said Picksniff, turning to leave.

"By the way, the derder collection is stored on the second floor, behind the grand staircase."

I looked up. There must have been fifty steps to the second floor. "Got it," I said. "Where's Randall?"

"Somewhere in this room," said Picksniff. "Even I don't know what his costume is. Now, please excuse me. I must attend to the guests. Perhaps the Goof Squad should mingle."

Goof Squad isn't our normal name.

But *mingle* is a normal word that means to mix with the crowd. It's also a detective word, meaning to pretend to be normal but knowing you're not. You need to have your eyes and ears open to discover bad guys.

We waded into the party just as a lady dressed like a striped cat and a man in a robot suit danced across the floor in front of us.

A wild laugh came from the food table, where two caped guys in yellow construction helmets told jokes. Not far away from them was a trio of skinny women, all lifting purple face masks to eat slices of cheese.

I was getting super-hungry, but we had a job to do, so I opened my cluebook to the sketch of the Dutchman and looked around.

"He doesn't seem to be here yet," I said.

"Cheese!" said a voice. We turned to a young man holding a silver tray of little foods. "Would the three of you like cheese?"

"What about me?" said Kelly, rustling her foil right in front of him.

The young man jumped back. "Where did *you* come from?" he asked.

"Nowhere," said Kelly. "And *every*where!"

Then she swiped a handful of cheese bits and vanished before I could congratulate her on her great line. But I wrote it down:

InvisiGirl: nowhere . . . and everywhere!

"Hot dogs in puffy dough!" gasped Mara at a passing tray. "See you heroes later!"

"But what about mingling?" I said.

"I'm mingling with that tray!" said Mara.

After she hustled away, Brian nudged my elbow. "That leaves Tommy Papers and Elbow Johnny. Ready, E.J.?" he asked.

"Ready," I said. "Now . . . mingle!"

We mingled like professional minglers who had won mingling awards from mingle societies. From group to group we went. We smiled. We hovered. We listened. We nodded. We mingled some more.

And we saw lots of strange people.

A man dressed like a bird with a name badge that read DOGMAN.

Three tiny boys dressed as babies with long gray beards who said they were twins.

Then we mingled with a short old man dressed in a green cape and a green mask and green gloves and green boots.

"Call me . . . ," he said in an old man's voice.

"Green Man?" Brian said.

"Red Boy," said the old man, hobbling away and shaking his head. "No one gets it. No one."

I wrote them all down in one word:

"Hey, E.J.," said Brian, "either we're going in circles or we've passed four different people in the same outfit."

I looked. I saw four ninja commandos, all in black jumpsuits, all wearing black masks and hoods. They were in different parts of the room and didn't look as if they were together.

"Let's keep an eye on them," I said.

"I feel as if someone has an eye on *us*," said Brian. "And by *us*, I mean you and Tommy Papers."

He was right. No matter where we mingled in the big room, I couldn't shake the feeling that we were being watched.

"Maybe those old crusty paintings are looking at us," I said, pointing to the wall.

Brian shivered. "That reminds me of a movie I saw once. It really scared me until . . . until . . ." He stopped.

I shivered. "Until what?" I asked.

"Until the movie ended, of course," Brian said. "I wasn't scared after that."

"But are you hungry?" I asked.

"More and more," he said.

My theory was working out. I wrote everything in my cluebook:

Eyes in paintings
Four ninja commandos
Brian being goofy (and hungry)

"Nobody's made a move up the grand staircase," he whispered.

I felt the tingle of mystery.

"Until now. Look!" I said as a glimpse of green flashed up the stairs to the second floor.

"It's Green Man!" I said.

"Or is it Red Boy?" asked Brian.

"Or is it . . . the Dutchman?" I said. "InvisiGirl! Blazey Blazington! After him!"

I elbowed my way through the crowd.

"Ow!"

"Hey!"

"Watch those skinny elbow bones, fella!"

"Tommy Papers scatters papers behind him," said Brian, scribbling like mad and tossing papers over his shoulders.

"No one's following *us*," I said. "We're following *the green guy*!"

Kelly was the first one up the stairs. We followed her into a maze of hallways.

Without Picksniff or Randall there, we got incredibly lost in the second-floor hallways.

I last saw Kelly darting down the hall ahead of us, but the instant we turned the corner, we saw—

No one!

"Where did she go?" asked Blazey.

Brian gasped "She really *is* InvisiGirl!"

Kelly was . . . gone!

5

In the Secret Room

"Kelly? Kelly! No!" said Mara. "She actually became invisible. I've lost my friend!"

We searched every inch of the hallway. There was no sign of anyone but us.

"Sure Kelly's InvisiGirl," I said. "But she's also an A-plus Goofball. And Goofballs stick together . . . so where . . . did she . . . go?"

I leaned up against the wall at the end of the hall.

All at once, a panel shifted.

"What's this?" I said. But before I knew it—*slooooop!*—the panel slid aside and I fell on my elbows.

Then Brian and Mara fell on me!

A second later, a pair of hands reached down to help us up. They were green hands attached to green arms attached to a green body, a green cape, a green hood, and a green mask.

"Green Man!" I cried.

"Red Boy!" said the voice. "Or, as I like to call myself . . . Randall Crandall!"

And the green mask slipped off to reveal none other than the goofy host of the party himself.

"Randall Crandall!" Brian said.

"None other," he said with a big smile. "And you found my secret passage. And me."

"And me!" said Kelly, who suddenly appeared on the far side of a room crammed with televisions and desks.

Brian blinked at all the equipment. "This is such a cool place. I could live here!"

"Sometimes I do," said Randall. "And I have, ever since I heard the Dutchman might try to steal my collection. I've been watching everything from this room."

"What do you call it?" I asked.

"My spy center," Randall said, sitting in front of the screens and adjusting some knobs. We saw directly into the ballroom below.

"Hey," said Mara. "The cameras are looking through the eyes of the paintings."

Randall grinned. "I needed to see what was going on. I'm glad you're here with me."

"Where exactly is *here*?" Kelly asked.

"The very center of my house," said Randall. "For anyone but a trained Goofball, it's nearly impossible to find my secret room. Anyone else would have to discover the exact sequence of rooms in order to find us. If you don't enter the rooms in the right order, you'll never find the treasure. Come, let me show you my collection."

He pressed a button on the desk, and the wall behind us shifted to reveal a bigger room, filled with display cases of derders.

"This is sooooo awesome," said Kelly.

Smiling, Randall lifted a glass case and took out a pair of connected tubes and another that was only an inch long from end to end.

"Here is the legendary double derder of Samarkand," he said. "While this is the collapsible derder favored by world travelers."

Fwip! The short derder expanded to over a foot long. When he breathed into it, a high soft note filled the room.

Brian's jaw hung open. His eyes glowed. "Ingenious!"

Randall smiled. "When my grandmother moved to Hawaii, she entrusted the entire collection to me. She warned me that the Dutchman might come one day to steal the world's largest collection of world-class derders in the world from me!"

"You said words two and three times," said Mara.

"The collection is that big," said Randall. "Look." He held up a tube covered in cloth, like a mummy.

"This early Egyptian model was discovered in the tomb of King Tut. The derder is fragile, of course, but it still works."

He blew gently into it.

Whooooo . . .

It was hypnotic.

Then he stepped to a large display case and tipped up its lid. He drew out a pillow on which lay a crudely carved wooden derder.

Kelly frowned "That one looks like a hollowed-out log."

"It looks like a hollowed-out log because it *is* a hollowed-out log," Randall said. "This was made by a young Abraham Lincoln."

"Holy cow!" said Brian. "I love that guy. And his hat."

"Which is essentially a fat derder closed on one end with a brim on the other. This other one," Randall said, pointing to a derder with an arrow through it, "is nearly as famous. It's Custer's Last Derder."

"This is like a museum," said Kelly.

Randall nodded at Kelly, then blinked at her outfit. "I bet after you used all that foil, you had quite a few derders yourself."

Kelly smiled. "Thirteen," she said.

Randall Crandall's eyes took on a faraway look. "Wow . . ."

"You can say that again," I said without thinking.

But we didn't do Rock, Paper, Scissors. We just let Randall say it again.

"Wow . . . ," he said.

"We should get back to the party," I said.

We left the hidden room through the maze of rooms that protected his collection.

First there was a personal bowling alley, then a private movie theater, then a Ping-Pong room, and lastly an ice-cream parlor.

Finally, we were on the balcony again, overlooking the crowded party.

"For a job this size," Randall said, "it's likely the Dutchman will have henchmen."

"*Henchmen* is a detective word," Kelly said to Brian. "It means evil bad guys who help a super-evil bad guy. I hope the Dutchman doesn't have too many hench—"

All at once—*zzzzt!*—we heard a strange buzzing sound from the ballroom below.

One of the ninja commandos looked up from his plate of little hot dogs. At the same moment, two other heads went up across the room. They were the heads of two other ninja commandos!

"It's a signal!" I whispered.

The three commandos rushed to the grand staircase and ran up.

"Where's the fourth ninja commando?" Mara asked.

All at once, *click*! The ceiling opened directly above us, and the fourth ninja commando slid down right in front of us!

6

The Dutchman's Henchmen!

Before we could move, the ninja henchman darted down the hallway toward the maze of rooms leading to the derders.

"Oh no!" said Randall. "After him!"

As we turned to chase the ninja commando, the three other ninja henchmen bounded up the other end of the hall and started chasing us.

"Now what?" asked Mara.

"Tommy knows!" said Brian. "It's paper time!" He quickly scribbled notes.

One said, *". . . the treasure is . . ."*

Another said, *". . . in the . . ."*

Tommy Papers scattered the notes behind him in little bits. Here, there, everywhere.

The plan worked perfectly, because as we chased the first henchman, the other three followed the fluttering papers.

"Now we go after the first guy!" said Kelly.

We zigzagged through the maze after the first henchman. "If I can get in front of him, I'll Blazey him!"

Suddenly, the ninja ducked into the ice-cream parlor. Maybe the guy was lucky, maybe he knew the way, but once we followed him into the parlor, he leaped over the counter as if it were nothing at all.

"Jumping is a good power!" said Brian.

As we leaped over the counter, the henchman dived through the nearest door and right into the Ping-Pong room!

"Uh-oh," said Randall. "He knows!"

But maybe he didn't.

In the Ping-Pong room, the bad guy darted this way and that, as if he couldn't decide which door to choose.

"You're trapped!" said Kelly popping up out of nowhere right behind him.

"And now I blaze!" said Mara.

The henchman's head spun from side to side when Mara twirled.

While he was dizzy, I raised my elbows and leaped at him, but the robber ducked the terrible wrath of my elbows and tumbled under the table and back across the room.

All at once—*wham!*—the door behind him opened and the three other henchmen followed him in. They were an army of four.

"We must stop them!" said Randall.

"We will!" said Kelly. "Arm yourselves!"

We each scooped up a Ping-Pong paddle and shot balls at the bad guys as if we were human machine guns.

It was a madhouse. While we pelted the henchmen, the one from the ceiling jumped from door to door, trying to choose the right one. There was only one way to catch him.

"Time for . . . Elbow Johnny!"

My elbows began swinging. I didn't know if it would work, but it sure looked deadly.

And weird. I caught a reflection of myself in InvisiGirl's costume. Those crazy elbows!

Suddenly, one of the bad guys hit the light switch, and the room went dark.

Squeak . . . whoosh!

Randall flicked the lights on as soon as he could, but every henchman was gone! The door to the movie theater was wide open!

"They slipped through my elbows," I said.

"Most things do," said Brian.

We slid into the movie theater. It was pitch black in there. We tiptoed down the aisle.

"This is the third room," Mara whispered. "One more, and they'll find the—"

Thump! Thump!

Three henchmen rushed at us from different parts of the theater. We each ran into a different row of seats.

"We have them on the run," said Kelly.

"I think they have *us* on the run," I said.

"Either way, there's a lot of running going on," said Mara.

"Except watch this!" whispered Brian. "Goofballs, into the shadows!"

We dived into the shadows along the walls.

Tommy Papers scattered notes all along one row. They were visible to all three robbers. Then Tommy ducked into the shadows with us.

One robber picked up one note, read it, and ran toward us. The robber in the next row picked up his note and ran toward us. The third one did the same. They all reached for the last note, which was just outside the shadows. All of a sudden, Brian snatched it away, and all three slammed into one another.

WHAMMM!

"Aha!" Randall cheered. "Got you!"

Except all at once, their buzzers went off.

"I have the derders!" called the fourth henchman, rushing into the theater with a big sack over his shoulder.

"Noooo!" cried Randall. "My collection!"

"How did he get in there?" I asked.

The four henchmen rushed at us, and in a single leap, they jumped over our heads and ran out of the theater.

We chased them, first through the Ping-Pong room, then through the ice-cream parlor, and finally down the hallway to the stairs leading to the ballroom.

As if nothing could stop them, the four henchmen tumbled down the giant stairs, leaped to their feet, and bolted out the far end of the room to the patio.

"Stop them!" cried Randall Crandall. "They're escaping across the lawn!"

7

The Lure of the Lawn

Because it was a warm night, the party had spilled outside. The back lawn was crowded with hundreds of weird superheroes, eating, chatting, and dancing under the lights strung from tree to tree all around the yard.

"Wow, a fairyland!" said Mara when we slid out to the patio.

"You can say that . . . once," I said.

"It looks like a city park," said
Kelly.

"It's actually bigger," said Randall.

"Which is great, except the four
henchmen disappeared into the
crowd," I said.

"Tommy doesn't see them
anywhere!" said Brian.

"They won't get far,'" said Randall.
"The yard has a super-high wall around
it."

"How long would it take them to get
to the wall?" Kelly asked.

Randall scratched his nose. "The
yard extends to Canada, so it could be a
few days."

I gave him a look. "We need to speed this up. Goofballs, we must employ THE GOOFBALL SYSTEM FOR FINDING CLUES. Except that this time we're looking for ninja robber henchmen commandos."

"I think the proper order is ninja commando robber henchmen," said Kelly.

"Them!" I said. "Let's go!"

The four Goofballs split up. We each took one side of the big backyard. We didn't put our noses to the ground. That would be messy. But we kept our eyes and ears open.

Randall came with me as we crept from group to group. No one had seen any ninjas or commandos or robbers or henchmen.

"This is terrible," Randall said. "My derder collection is lost!"

I felt bad for him. I didn't know what to say. We had failed him. We had failed to solve the mystery in time.

Then, as if he had heard his best friend, Randall's pony, Thunder, trotted over from the crowd. Behind him, he drew a cart piled high with cheesy snacks for the guests.

"Thunder, what are we going to do?" said Randall, petting Thunder's neck. "Grandma will be so sad." He turned to me. "Grandma gave me both the collection and Thunder."

I didn't know that. But I understood what he was feeling. And I felt sad, too.

As Randall let Thunder continue his round of the backyard, Brian, Kelly, and Mara finished their sniffing and found us.

"We didn't find them, either," Mara said.

"It's like they all just vanished," I said.

"Without aluminum foil, too," Kelly added.

We watched as some of the silly superheroes gathered around a troupe of jugglers in striped outfits doing tricks. The people clapped. When the jugglers stood on each other's shoulders, the crowd cheered even more.

"The acrobats are standing pretty high up there," said Brian. "Tommy wonders if they saw anything from up there."

"I guess we can ask them," said Randall with a sigh. "Wait a second. Acrobats? I didn't invite any acrobats!"

I flipped through my cluebook. I saw one of my very earliest clues.

All of a sudden, I realized something.

"The ninjas must have changed into acrobat outfits. People, those acrobats *are* the henchmen commando robbers!" I cried.

Without waiting for the order of the words to be corrected, I raced over to them. Three acrobats were now doing cartwheels across the grass, jumping over one another, and getting farther and farther from the house.

"Where's the fourth one?" asked Kelly.

"There!" said Brian, pointing to the fourth henchman, trying to sneak away from the crowd with a big sack over his shoulder.

"Go, Elbow Johnny, go!" cried Mara.

I rushed over, my elbows swinging wildly. The robber didn't stand a chance. Even after he fell backward, I didn't stop swinging.

"Cease the elbows!" the robber yelled. "You're just plain nutty!"

"We caught you derder-handed," said Kelly as Randall wrestled the sack of stolen derders from the henchman's gloved hands.

He opened the sack and gasped.

"These derders aren't from my collection. These derders are from . . . my bathroom!"

He emptied the sack of regular cardboard tubes onto the lawn.

Mara stood over the henchman, glaring down through her big green glasses at the masked face. "Prepare to be identified!"

Then she whipped off the ninja's mask.

And long red hair poured down.

"What?" I gasped.

The other henchmen took off their masks. The henchmen weren't hench*men* at all. They weren't even hench*boys*.

"They're hench*girls*!" said Kelly.

In fact, the lead henchgirl was Millie Carlson. The captain of the middle-school gymnastic team. She flipped her red hair to the other side of her head.

"Why are you so evil?" Randall asked.

Millie blinked. "I'm not evil. My teachers like me lots."

"Then why are you trying to steal Randall Crandall's derder collection?" I asked.

"Steal?" Millie said. "I'm not stealing. All we were supposed to do was run around the house doing tricks and then run away."

"Who told you to do this?" I asked.

"The gymnastics team got a call, inviting us to the party," Millie said.

"Not from me," said Randall. Suddenly, he gasped. "The Dutchman! How perfectly diabolical! But why lure us all the way out here for a sack of fake derders?"

"To distract us?" said Kelly. "Because the real robbery is—"

"Master Randall and the Goofbabies!" came a yell from the house.

We turned to see Picksniff racing across the lawn to us. "The Dutchman is here!" he cried.

All at once, we heard the sound of a pony whinnying loudly.

"Thunder?" said Randall.

"Yee-haw!" shouted a voice.

Everyone turned.

Riding Thunder's cart was a person wearing a big floppy hat who also had a big curly mustache flying in the wind.

"It's the Dutchman!" we shouted.

The Opposite of
Dutch

"My grandmother told me about you, Dutchman!" Randall yelled. "You'll never steal my treasure!"

We chased the Dutchman over the lawn, across the patio, and straight through the open doors into the ballroom.

We were a super-goofy team in action.

I swung my elbows swiftly to get us through the crowd.

"Oooh! Hey! Oww! Oh!"

"Tommy—will—get—the—
Dutchman! Dutchman!" Brian cried,
and Tommy Papers tossed crumpled
notes all over the place.

It looked like crazy litter, but the
Dutchman couldn't help himself.
He pulled the reins to slow Thunder,
grabbed the notes, and read them.

"Tommy knew the Dutchman was a
reader!" Brian said.

The Dutchman growled under his
floppy hat. "But what does this mean?
These papers make no sense!"

"Enough sense to stop you!" Tommy
said with a laugh.

Then, unseen by everyone, InvisiGirl
appeared on the cart next to the
Dutchman and wrestled the reins away
from him.

"Where did *you* come from?" shrieked the Dutchman.

"Nowhere . . . and *everywhere!*" Kelly exclaimed. "And now, Dutchman, your plans are foiled. Aluminum foiled!"

Kelly jiggled her foil mirrors, and the Dutchman tried to look away. But Blazey Blazington was there, spinning like a top.

The Dutchman, confused by the kaleidoscope of colors, got dizzy and tumbled off the cart into a big bouquet of flowers, which Thunder was munching.

Before the Dutchman could escape, I leaped over to him, pointed my elbows in different directions, and let them fly.

The Dutchman couldn't decide which way to escape.

"Trapped!" we all said together.

The Dutchman climbed slowly to his feet and stood, wobbling. His face was hidden in the shadow of a big floppy hat. Just like in the photograph.

Just like in my cluebook sketch.

"You captured my henchmen," he said.

"They were good," I said. "But they weren't Goofballs."

"Alas, no," said the Dutchman.

"Now, off with the disguise," said Kelly.

The Dutchman sighed heavily.

Then the mustache came off.

The sunglasses came off.

The floppy hat came off.

Suddenly, Brian gasped. "You aren't a Dutchman at all! In fact you're the opposite."

The Dutchman was . . . a woman, an older woman with white hair and a big smile.

Kelly blinked. "I know the opposite of a man is a woman. But what's the opposite of Dutch?"

Randall Crandall came running over.
"I'll tell you," he said. "It's GRAMMY!"

Then he threw his arms around the
smiling woman.

"Grammy, *you're* the Dutchman?"

"I am," said Grammy.

"You made me think my collection was going to be stolen," said Randall.

"I did," Grammy said.

"But why?"

The white-haired woman smiled. "Because I needed to know that your collection was safe. And it is. If you —and your friends—could foil— aluminum foil—someone as clever as a grandma, it was worth it."

Randall scratched his nose. "Worth what? Why did you want to know if the collection was safe?"

"It needs to be safe," Grammy said. "Because today you get . . . a new derder."

Randall jumped. "A new one? Really?"

From under her Dutchman cloak, Randall's grandmother produced a long shiny tube.

"It's . . . beautiful," whispered Randall.

It *was* beautiful. Long and tapered at one end, the derder was encrusted with jewels that glowed under the light of the chandelier.

"Behold, the legendary Maltese Derder," she said. Then, holding it to her lips, she let out a long breath.

Derrr—der—eeee—rrrrrr!

It was the most amazing sound.

"It was said to belong to Cleopatra, Queen of Egypt," Grammy said. "From there it surfaced in the court of King Arthur at Camelot.

"George Washington even had it for a short time. I finally tracked it down at a pancake house in Africa. And now it comes . . . to you."

Randall Crandall closed his eyes. When he opened them again, they were wet with tears. "Thank you, Grammy. It's the second most valuable derder in my collection," he said.

"What's the most valuable?" asked Brian.

Randall grinned, then walked to the far wall. Stepping on his tiptoes, he breathed into a tube there.

Everyone hushed to hear the low mellow sound. The whole room sounded like the inside of a trumpet.

"It's the longest derder I've ever seen," said Kelly.

"That's because it's the world's longest derder in the world!" said Randall. "I made it by connecting wrapping-paper tubes end to end. And I keep adding to it year after year. After every party, after every holiday, I add more derders to it. It never stops growing!"

"What a Goofball," I said to Randall.

He smiled. "I like to think so."

"Mystery solved!" said Brian.

"Except there's one more Goofball mystery to solve," said Randall with a sly smile.

"There is?" said Kelly. "What mystery?"

Randall blew into the derder a second time, the front doors swung wide open, and in walked Luigi the baker, his arms filled with giant pizza boxes.

"The mystery topping!" Mara gasped.

We all raced over. We flipped open the top box. The Anniversary Goofball Pizza had *five* toppings.

Cheese.

Garlic.

Pineapple.

Peanut Butter. And . . .

"Mango!" I shouted, ripping off a slice.

"I love mango!" said Mara, taking another slice.

"You love every food!" said Kelly, taking a third slice.

"Me, too!" said Randall, taking a fourth slice.

"Me, three!" said Grammy, taking a fifth slice.

"Me, four!" said Millie, taking a sixth slice.

"Myself, as well," said Picksniff, taking a seventh slice.

"Neigh!" said Thunder, taking the eighth slice.

"Mmmmrfffrrmmm!" said Brian, stuffing four more slices into his mouth.

Proving what I always suspected.

Goofballs are the goofiest when they're hungry!